Big Bear
Little Bear

For Deborah
~ *DB*

For Noah who is little, and
for Jake who wants to be BIG
~ *JC*

This edition produced 2004 for
READER'S CHOICE BOOKS
50 E. Burlington Avenue, Fairfield, Iowa 52556 by
LITTLE TIGER PRESS
An imprint of Magi Publications
1 The Coda Centre, 189 Munster Road, London SW6 6AW, UK
www.littletigerpress.com
First published in the United States 2001
by Handprint Books
Originally published in Great Britain 2001
Text © 2001 David Bedford • Illustrations © 2001 Jane Chapman
Printed in Singapore • ISBN 1 84506 141 1
1 3 5 7 9 10 8 6 4 2

Big Bear
Little Bear

DAVID BEDFORD AND JANE CHAPMAN

LITTLE TIGER PRESS

One bright cold morning Little Bear helped Mother Bear scoop snow out of their den. "This will make more room for you to play," said Mother Bear. "You're getting bigger now."

"I want to be as big as you when I'm grown up,"
said Little Bear. He stretched up his arms and
made himself as big as he could.

Mother Bear stretched to the sky.
"You'll have to eat and eat to be
as big as I am," she said.
"When I'm big, I'll wrestle you
in the snow," said Little Bear.
Wrestling in the snow was
his favorite game.

"You're not big enough to wrestle me yet,"
said Mother Bear, laughing.
She rolled Little Bear over and over in
the soft snow and Little Bear giggled.

Little Bear shook the snow from his fur.
"When I'm grown up I want to run as
fast as you, Mommy," he said.
"You'll have to practice if you want to
be as fast as I am," said Mother Bear.

Little Bear darted away and
ran as fast as he could . . .

but his mother soon caught up with him.
"Run faster!" she called.
"I can't," said Little Bear. "I'm not grown
up yet."

"I'll show you what it's like to be grown up," said Mother Bear. "Climb onto my shoulders!" When Little Bear stood on his mother's shoulders he could see to the end of the world, and when he reached up his hands he could nearly touch the sky. "Now you *are* big," said Mother Bear.

"Let's run," cried Mother Bear, and she
ran faster and faster.
Little Bear felt the wind rushing against
his face and blowing his ears back.
"This is how I'll run when I'm grown up,"
he shouted.

Suddenly, Mother Bear leapt into the air.
Little Bear saw the world rushing under him.
"I'm flying like a bird," he shouted.
Then he saw where they were going to land . . .

SPLASH!

Mother Bear dove into the cold water and swam along with Little Bear on her back. "This is how you'll swim when you're grown up," she said.

Little Bear watched his mother
carefully so he would know
what to do next time.
"I'll soon be able to swim like
that," he told himself.

Mother Bear climbed out of the water with Little Bear still clinging tightly to her back. "Will I *really* be as big as you when I'm grown up?" asked Little Bear.

"Yes you will," said his mother— "but I don't want you to grow up yet." "Why not?" asked Little Bear.

"You won't be able to sit on my shoulders when you're grown up," said Mother Bear, as she carried Little Bear back to their snow den.

Little Bear was tired after wrestling,
running, flying, and swimming.
"You can still cuddle me when
I'm grown up," he said, sleepily.
"But Mommy," he whispered,
"I don't want to grow up yet."

"That's good," said Mother Bear,
holding him close, "because . . .

you're perfect just the way
you are."
Little Bear snuggled into his
mother's soft fur, and they
went to sleep together in
their cozy den in the snow.